O LITTLE TOWN

Tana Reiff

A Pacemaker® **HOPES** *And* **DREAMS** Book

FEARON/JANUS/QUERCUS
Belmont, California

Simon & Schu

O Little Town

Tana Reiff
AR B.L.: 2.6
Points: 1.0

UG

HOPES *And* DREAMS

Cover photo: Library of Congress
Illustration: Tennessee Dixon

ISBN 0-8224-3681-7
Library of Congress
Catalog Card Number: 87-83214
Printed in the United States of America
10 9 8 7
MA

CONTENTS

CHAPTER 1
Germany, 1852

Karl Hermann
sat at his school desk.
He looked up
at the map
on the wall.
He studied
the shape
of the young country
called America.
He saw
only lines and colors.
He wondered
what America
was really like.

All the Germans
talked about America.
They read books
about America.

They heard stories
about America.
Some Germans
even went there.
These people
did not wish
to leave dear Germany.
But each year
German life
was getting harder.
Harvests were poor.
Many Germans were hungry
and out of work.

No longer
could people cut wood
from any forest.
The state
took all the wood.
They used it
for the factories
and the railroad.

The factories
made things
faster than by hand.

But now
things cost much more.

The farms
were cut up
into pieces.
Karl's father had to
use every inch of land.
Still, the farm
was too small.

Then there was
Uncle Ludwig.
He made hats.
The factories
put him out of business.
He moved to the city
and went to work
in a factory.
He hated
the hot, dirty factory.
He hated the city.

"What will you be
when you grow up?"
asked the teacher.

Karl snapped
out of his dream.
"I want to be
a farmer
in America,"
he answered.

"Not a German farmer?"
the teacher asked.

"I will always be
a German,"
said Karl.
"But the farms in Germany
are too small.
I want a big farm
in America."

"You have
a big dream,"
said the teacher.
"You had better
study hard.
A good life
comes only to those
who work hard."

Thinking It Over

1. Do you believe
   in dreams?

2. Is hard work
   the only way
   to a good life?

3. Is there a place
   you would like
   to see sometime?

CHAPTER 2

"Uncle Ludwig
has something to say,"
said Karl's mother.

"I cannot live
in the city,"
said Uncle Ludwig.
"I am going
to America.
I will leave
next week.
I will write to you."

Karl was sad.
He loved his uncle.
He loved
Uncle Ludwig's stories.
He loved
to hear him sing.
Might he never again
see his uncle?

Karl and his three sisters
said goodbye
to Uncle Ludwig.
Karl wiped a tear
from his eye.

"Can we go, too?"
Karl asked his father.

"It is not so easy,"
said Mr. Hermann.
"This is our land.
This is our home."

But a few months later
Karl's father died.
Karl left school.
He and his sisters
helped to run
the little farm.
To make ends meet,
Karl also worked
with wood.
It was not possible
to go to America now.

All the while,
Karl read
about America.
"There are
miles and miles
of open land,"
said one book.
"The animals
are fat
and full of meat.
The hills
are green.
There are
many German people there.
They are building
clean towns.
America is a fine land
for a good German life."

And there were
Uncle Ludwig's letters
from America.
He lived
in Milwaukee, Wisconsin.
He ran
a little hat shop

in town.
He did not make hats.
But he sold
a lot of them.
He was a happy man.

   "Come to Wisconsin,"
Uncle Ludwig wrote.
"If you want a farm,
this is the place.
And here in Wisconsin,
you can vote
after just one year!"

   Karl longed to see
his Uncle Ludwig.
He could almost feel
the black earth
of Wisconsin.
Life in Germany
was only getting worse.

Thinking It Over

1. What is the difference
   between hearing a story
   and reading a letter?

2. Do you think
   Karl will ever see
   his Uncle Ludwig?

CHAPTER **3**

Karl Hermann
grew up.
He married
a girl named Greta.
His mother
had died.
The little farm
was now his.

"I am 23 years old,"
Karl said to Greta.
"We are strong.
We have
some money put away.
The war
between the states
is over.
They are
almost giving away land
in the United States.
I have always

wanted to go
to America.
Now is the time."

"But Germany
is our home,"
said Greta.

"Yes, it is,"
said Karl.
"And I do not like
leaving our land.
But there is
no hope here.
There is great hope
in America.
Like my father,
I am a smart farmer.
I know how to farm
up and down the hills.
I grow
two or three crops a year
in every little field.
How much more
can I do
with only ten acres?

In America,
we can have
a fine, big farm.
But we will always
be German."

So Karl learned
all about the ships
going to America.
He picked the best one.

Greta packed a chest.
She packed food.
She packed her violin.
She wrapped up the bow
and some violin strings.

And she packed
their favorite Christmas tree ball.
It was gold.
It had
a beautiful shine.
"This will help us
remember Christmas
in Germany,"
said Greta.

Thinking It Over

1. How much
   do you plan
   before you go away?

2. What favorite thing
   would you pack
   to take
   to a new home?

3. How important
   is music to you?

CHAPTER **4**

The young pair
set off for France.
There, they would
meet their ship.

They made the trip
in a covered wagon.
They ate
black bread and cheese.
At night,
they camped out
beside a small fire.
Greta played music
on her violin.

Karl and Greta
had to wait
in France
for a week.
At last,
the wind was right.

The ship
was ready to sail.
It was the ship
Karl had picked.

"Where are
the iron beds?"
asked Karl.
"We were told
there were iron beds
with clean sheets."

"No beds,"
said the ship's mate.
"No sheets.
See those boards
along the walls?
You sleep
on a board."

The trip
across the ocean
took two months.
People got sick.
People died.

There were fights
over food.

And there were
bad storms
at sea.
The waves crashed
into the ship.
The wind screamed
in the night.
The children screamed
in their sleep.
Greta played her violin
to make them feel better.

Finally one morning,
the ship
pulled into New York.

Thinking It Over

1. Can you stand
   a hard trip
   if it gets you
   where you want to go?

2. What would you
   be thinking about
   if you had just arrived
   in a strange, new country?

CHAPTER 5

Karl and Greta
stepped off the ship.
"So this is America!"
Karl said.
"Which way
to Wisconsin?"

They went
by train
and then by boat.
They crossed
New York State.
They crossed
Lake Michigan.
At last they came
to Milwaukee, Wisconsin.
There they found
Uncle Ludwig's hat store.

Uncle Ludwig
welcomed Karl and Greta

with open arms.
"Live with me!"
he begged.

"We will stay
with you,"
said Karl.
"But only until
we find some land."

Uncle Ludwig
told stories
about life in Milwaukee.
He had made
many new friends.
Most of them
were German.

Then one day
Karl spotted a sign.
It said:
160 acres of land
$1.25 an acre!
Must stay five years.
Become a citizen
and the land is yours!

"We can't
buy this land,"
said Karl.
"We are German.
We will always
be German."

"But how else
can we get
160 acres?"
asked Greta.
"Think of it!
What a fine farm
we could have!
We must go
and look at it."

"All right,"
said Karl.
"We will go and see
what is out there.
We will go
and find ourselves some land."

Thinking It Over

1. Would you
   become a citizen
   for a good land deal?
   Why or why not?

2. Are you willing
   to give a new idea
   a chance?

CHAPTER 6

Uncle Ludwig
was sad
when Karl and Greta left.
But they had to go.

They went north
along Lake Michigan.
Soon they came
to the land
that was for sale.

"I can't do it!"
said Karl.
"I am German,
not American.
I cannot take
this land.
I cannot say
that I will become a citizen.
We will have to find
another place."

Karl and Greta
found a small farm
to buy.
The people
were heading west.
The farm needed
a lot of work.

"How can they leave
this place?"
Karl wondered.
"How could they let it
get so run-down?
Have they no love
for the land?"

But there was
something beautiful
about this farm.
The earth
was rich and black.
The air
was fresh and clean.
Much of the land
was still forest.

"Lots of trees
mean good earth,"
said Karl.
And there were also
rolling hills
and a stream.

"It looks
like Germany!"
said Karl.
"It looks
like home!"

Karl remembered
how the forests
in Germany
had been cut down.
That had made
his family angry.
Now he and Greta
had a forest
all to themselves.
They would clear
only the land
they needed.

The first year
they fixed up
the farmhouse.
They planted wheat
and other crops.
They fixed up
the old log house.
And they had
their first child.
Her name was Liesl.

By the next year
they got some animals.
They had two chickens,
three milk cows,
four pigs,
and five sheep.
They also had
a team of horses.

The year after that,
they had a son.
His name was Dieter.

Hundreds of Germans
lived all around.

They got together often
to sing and drink beer.

"Here's a drink
for my new son!"
said Karl one night.

All the Germans
lifted their glasses.

"To my son, Dieter!"
Karl began.
"May he always stay on
our dear family farm!"

"Here, here!"
said the crowd.

"And to us!"
Karl went on.
"May we always
stay German!"

They tapped glasses.
Then they sang
another German song.

Thinking It Over

1. Why is it important to Karl to "stay German"?

2. What has happened to many of the old family farms?

CHAPTER 7

Karl put the last nail
into the cow and horse barn.
"Finished!"
he shouted.

"Let's see
how the animals
like their new home,"
said Greta.

Liesl helped
to make beds
for the animals.
Dieter made sure
there was water
for them.
Then the cows and horses
stepped into the new barn.

"I have
big plans

29

for this farm,"
said Karl.

"You just finished
the barn!"
said Greta.

"Next we will build
a summer kitchen,"
Karl said.

"I could use
a nice big kitchen
to make my butter,"
said Greta.

By the next summer
the Hermanns had
three more buildings.
Greta loved
the summer kitchen.
She made
200 pounds of butter
the first year.
She made soap.
She baked bread.

The Hermanns
used their new smokehouse
to smoke meat.
Then they had meat
for the whole winter.

Under the springhouse
was a well.
The Hermanns
had all the clear spring water
they needed.

Liesl and Dieter
loved the farm.
They ran and played
all over.
Liesl picked wildflowers
in the summer.
Dieter gave names
to all the animals.

Greta was making
more butter
than the family needed.
"I should try
to sell some butter

in town,"
she said.

But she was afraid.
She had never
taken any farm goods
to town.

She set out
by herself
in the wagon.
She took along
a few pounds of butter.
She went
to her favorite store.

"Mr. Wagner,"
she began.
"Would you be able
to sell
some of my butter?
It's very good."

"I'll tell you what,"
said Mr. Wagner.
"You give me

your butter.
And you take
a dollar's worth
of things
from my store."

"You mean
we can trade?"
asked Greta.

"That's what I do
with the farmers,"
said Mr. Wagner.
"We trade
all sorts of things."

"All right, Mr. Wagner,"
said Greta.
"Let's trade."
They shook hands.

"We're in business!"
said Mr. Wagner.

Thinking It Over

1. Would you enjoy living on a farm like the Hermann's?

2. What do you think of trading goods?

CHAPTER 8

Three more years
went by.
The Hermanns
had another baby.
They called him Fritz.
The farm
was doing very well.

"This will be
our best Christmas ever!"
cried Liesl.

"Yes, child,"
said Karl.
"Let's go out
and cut a Christmas tree!"

Karl took a child
by each hand.
They walked out
into the snow.

"This one, this one!"
pointed Dieter.
"Make this one
our Christmas tree!"

Karl didn't cut
many trees.
But this was different.
It was a Christmas tree.
It fell to the ground.
Karl and the children
pulled it back
to the house.

The children
put candles
on the tree.
Then little Dieter
stood up on a chair.
He reached
to the top
of the tree.
He hung
the gold Christmas ball
from Germany.
It fit just right.

"Let's sing!"
said Karl.
The children sang.
Baby Fritz
clapped his hands.

Uncle Ludwig
came for dinner.
Greta and Liesl
cooked meat and vegetables
from the farm.

Then Uncle Ludwig
started singing Christmas songs
from Germany.
Everyone joined in.
Greta played along
on her violin.

"Silent night,
Holy night.
All is calm,
All is bright. . . ."

They sang
in German.

Dieter grabbed
for his mother's violin.
"I want to play,"
he said.

"I will teach you
when you are
a little older,"
said Greta.

"Now let's sing
'O Little Town',"
said Karl.

"We have
our own little town,"
said Dieter.

Karl and Greta
looked at each other.
They laughed.
They knew
the child was right.
The farm had become
their own little town.

Thinking It Over

1. Is Christmas
   a special time
   at your house?
   If so,
   what things
   do you do
   every year?

2. Do you sing
   or play an instrument?

3. Do you remember
   when you learned
   Christmas songs?

CHAPTER 9

The years flew by.
Greta looked
out the kitchen window.
She saw
Karl and the boys
walking toward the house.
They were finished working
for the day.
The boys
were tall and strong now.
Karl liked working
side by side
with his sons.

"This is good,"
Greta said to herself.
"The boys
are here on the farm.
And Liesl
teaches kindergarten
in the town school."

Karl and the boys
came into the house.
Greta and Liesl
put their dinner
on the table.

"The orchestra
from New York
is coming to Milwaukee,"
said Dieter.
"I would very much like
to go."

"Oh, how nice!"
said Greta.
"Let's get tickets!"
She had taught Dieter
to play the violin.
Over the years
he had become
very good at it.

"You and Dieter go,"
said Karl.
"And Liesl, too.
She's a singer.

She might like
to hear an orchestra
play fine German music.
My idea
of good music
is to sing drinking songs
at the beer hall!"

So Greta, Liesl, and Dieter
went to Milwaukee.
The orchestra played
beautiful music
that night.

"I don't want
to leave,"
said Dieter
at the end.
"I want to meet
the violin players."

He went back
to meet them.
"Someday I want
to join an orchestra,"
he told the players.

"Will you play
for us tonight?"
asked one of them.
"Here is my violin.
Show us
what you can do."

Dieter was shaking.
He put
the fine violin
under his neck.
He took the bow
in his other hand.
He could not believe
how beautiful
this violin sounded.
He did not see
the orchestra leader
walk up.

"Who is this boy?"
the orchestra leader asked.
"You are very good,
young man.
Very, very good.
We have

an open chair
in the strings.
Will you join
our orchestra?"

Dieter put down
the violin.
He knew
how sorry
his father would be.
It was Karl Hermann's dream
for his boys
to stay on the farm.
But it was Dieter's dream
to play
in a fine orchestra.

"Give us
your answer
by tomorrow,"
said the orchestra leader.
"We are heading
to Ohio.
You can come along.
We need you
right away."

Thinking It Over

1. Do you think
   it is important
   for the whole family
   to stay on the farm?

2. What happens
   when a parent's dream
   is different
   from a child's?

CHAPTER **10**

Dieter had been
with the orchestra
for five years.
He lived in New York.
But he played
all over the country.
Sometimes he came
to Milwaukee.
Karl never went
to hear the orchestra.

"And what
are we going to do
about you, Liesl?"
said Karl.
"You're still
not married!
You are too busy
teaching kindergarten
and singing
with your group!"

"I have always
loved to sing,"
said Liesl.
"In fact,
our singing group
is going to New York.
We will be going up
against other groups
from all over.
May I go?"

"New York
is a long way to go
just to sing,"
said Karl.

"I can also
visit Dieter,"
said Liesl.

"Are you afraid
she won't come back?"
asked Greta.

"I have
lost a son,"

said Karl.
"Maybe Liesl
will also go away."

"I'll come home!"
said Liesl.

"Don't worry,"
said Fritz.
"I'm here
to help you farm."

So Liesl
went to New York
with the singing group.
She stayed
with Dieter.
"Will you
come and listen?"
Liesl asked.
"You will bring me
good luck."

The big hall
was packed.
Dieter got a seat

right in front.
Liesl's group
sang beautiful old German songs.
They were very good.

"Your group
was great!"
said Dieter
after their turn.

"But who is the best?"
laughed Liesl.

They had to wait
for hours
to find out.

At last,
a man
began to call out winners.

"Won't they ever
say 'Milwaukee'?"
Liesl whispered.
"I guess
we didn't win."

"They are not
finished yet!"
said Dieter.

"Second place
goes to Milwaukee, Wisconsin!"
the man called.

Liesl jumped up.
"Not bad
for a bunch of farmers!"
Liesl laughed.
She and Dieter jumped
up and down together.

But the joy
did not last long.
Back at Dieter's,
there was a letter
waiting for them.

"Come home
right away!"
it said.
"Uncle Ludwig
has died."

Thinking It Over

1. Is there a time
   when children
   must leave home?

2. What have you
   ever won?

CHAPTER 11

All the Hermanns
met in Milwaukee.
Together they said goodbye
to Uncle Ludwig.
They watched
as the wood box
went into the ground.

After the service,
the Hermanns put out
lots of food.
A young man
walked over
to Karl and Liesl.

"My name
is Johann Schell,"
he said.
"I worked
in your uncle's hat shop.

I would like
to take over
the business."

"That would be fine,"
said Karl.

But Johann
was looking at Liesl.
And Liesl
was looking at Johann.

In just a few months,
Liesl and Johann
were married.
Again, the Hermanns
laid out lots of good food.

"I am happy
you found a fine husband,"
said Karl.
"But I am sad
that you will leave the farm."

"I'll just be
in Milwaukee,"

said Liesl.
"I'll help Johann
run Uncle Ludwig's business.
We will live
over the shop."

"I guess that Fritz
will leave one day, too,"
said Karl.

"I won't leave,"
said Fritz.
"I love the farm.
I want
to build it even more.
We will make this
the best milk farm
in Wisconsin!
We will turn out
cheese and butter and milk
like no other!"

"That's a fine dream,"
said Karl.
"But we are working
as much as we can."

"We must take on
new people,"
said Fritz.
"There is
lots of work here.
There is
lots of room to grow.
We will clear
more forest.
We can buy
100 new cows
right away!"

"That's my boy,"
said Karl.
"That's my boy."

Thinking It Over

1. Have you ever
   lost one thing
   and then got something else
   in its place?

2. What makes parents
   happy with their children?

CHAPTER **12**

Fritz and his father
walked past the milk plant.
Inside, 20 people
put milk into cans.
Outside the plant
were wagons.
Men loaded the cans.
Then they drove
the wagons to Milwaukee.

"Our little town
is not so little now,"
said Fritz.

"Your mother and I
have been here
for 50 years,"
said old Karl Hermann.
"I had big dreams.
But in my dreams
I never saw

the Hermann dairy.
I needed you
to carry on."

   "And my son Josef
will carry on
after both of us,"
said Fritz.

   It was time
for dinner.
The two men
walked toward the big house.
One of them
had some gray hair now.
The other's back
was bowed.
Time had a way
of showing its mark.

   "The United States
has joined
the Great War,"
said Karl
at dinner.
"American boys

are fighting
in Europe.
I am glad
we are still German."

"But I was born here,"
said Josef.
"I am American."

"What are you saying, boy?"
said his grandfather.

"I want to go
to Europe,"
said Josef.
"I want to fight
for the United States."

Karl was angry.
"The son of my son
wants to fight
against Germany?"
he asked.
"I say
we are German,
not American."

"How can you
still think like that?"
asked Fritz.

"And what about
the farm?"
asked Karl.
"We need Josef here."

"We will be OK
until Josef comes back,"
said Fritz.
"He can pick up
where he left off.
He wants to fight
for his country."

And so young Josef
went off to war.

Thinking It Over

1. In what ways
   can you tell
   that time has passed
   since you were very young?

2. Why do some older people
   hold on to old ideas?

3. Do you think the Hermanns
   are German or American?

CHAPTER **13**

Young Josef Hermann
was fighting
for the Americans.
He was fighting
in France
against the Germans.

Back home
there was trouble, too.
Some Americans
were afraid
of people with German names.
They stopped schools
from teaching German.
They stopped the printing
of German newspapers.
They changed the names
of streets with German names.

Then Liesl's singing group
got a letter.

"A group such as yours
is not American.
You sing
only German songs.
By doing so,
you are helping
the German cause.
You must break up
or face a big fight."

Liesl stood
before the group.
"What are we to do?"
she asked.
"We are Americans.
We just like
to sing German songs.
We are not helping Germany."

"I say
let's keep on singing!"
said Hans Menner.

"You don't know
these people,"
said his wife.

"They mean
what they say.
They can cause us
big problems.
They might even hurt
our families."

"I have not seen
people angry at Germans
since before the Civil War,"
said one old woman.

"Let's sing!
Let's sing!"
shouted others.
"We are doing
nothing wrong!
Christmas is coming.
Let's sing
'O Little Town'!"

The group
began to sing.
The song
made Liesl think
of her family's farm.

She remembered
how safe life was
when she was a girl.

She walked home alone.
The farm and young Josef
were on her mind.

As she got near,
she saw people
in the street.
They stood around
in front of the hat shop.
Then she saw policemen
in the crowd.

She ran
toward the shop.
"What is going on?"
she called.

Then she saw.
The front window
was smashed.
The little store sign
that read

"J. Schell Hats"
lay on the ground.

Johann came outside.
"See what they have done!"
he cried.

"Who? Who?"
asked Liesl.
But she knew.
"Why do some people
hate German-Americans?"
she asked.
"Why do they think
we side with the Germans?"

"They did not hurt us,"
said Johann.
"We can put in
a new window."

"Then we'll go
to the farm
for a few weeks,"
said Liesl.
"We should get away."

Thinking It Over

1. Do you believe
   the German-Americans
   were helping the Germans?

2. Is there ever a good reason
   to hurt people or things?

CHAPTER **14**

Johann went back
to Milwaukee.
He had to keep
the business going.

Liesl stayed on
at the farm.
Word came
that the singing group
broke up.
But Christmas
was just around the corner.
There was
food to make.
The men brought in
a fresh-cut Christmas tree.
And Liesl and her mother
were rolling bandages
for the Red Cross.

"How can anyone believe
we are helping
the Germans?"
asked Greta.
"Here we are,
helping our boys.
And Fritz is out
selling war bonds!"

"Do you know
what I heard?"
asked Liesl.
"They are saying
we roll ground glass
into the bandages!"

"Oh, no!"
said Greta.

Fritz knocked
on the door
of an old German farmer.
"Would you like
to help the U.S.?"
Fritz asked.

"Buy a war bond.
Help us win the war!"

"I'm German,"
said the farmer.
He banged the door
in Fritz's face.

That night
the family
was putting up
the Christmas tree.

"What do you think
of that old man?"
Fritz asked Karl.

"He makes me angry,"
said Karl.
"I may be German.
But I want the U.S.
to win this war!
That German farmer
should not act that way
to another German."

"But what are you, Father?"
asked Fritz.
"German or American?"

Just then
there was a knock
at the door.
Greta got up
to answer it.

Standing there
was a tall man.
The letters "U.S."
were on his coat.
"Is this the home
of Josef Hermann?"
he asked.

"Yes,"
said Greta, slowly.

"I am sorry
to have to tell you this,"
he began.
"Josef Hermann

has been killed.
He died in battle
in France.
He died
for his country."

Greta cried.
Josef's mother
fell into Fritz's arms.
Karl's face dropped.
Liesl came over
to help her mother.

"The body
will be sent home
as soon as possible,"
said the tall man.

Karl looked at Fritz.
Softly he said,
"Our boy died
fighting for our country."

"What did you say?"
Fritz asked.

"I said, 'our country,'"
said Karl.
"I want to go see
that old German farmer.
I want
to speak my piece.
Right now!
Drive me over, Fritz!"

Fritz got out
the wagon.
Off they went.

"You say
you are German,"
Karl said to the farmer.
"Now let me tell you
a few things.
I was born
in Germany, too.
But my farm
is in Wisconsin, U.S.A.
My cows
eat off American earth.
Here in Wisconsin,

my wife and I
raised a family.
And my son's son
died for the U.S.
So you see,
I must be American.
What else
can I be?
Listen to me say this:
I am an American.
Now do you see
why my son
is selling war bonds?"

Then Fritz and Karl
went home.
There was still time
to finish the Christmas tree.

"Where is
that old gold ball?"
asked Karl.

Greta handed it to him.

      "This ball
has seen Christmas in America
more than 50 times,"
Karl said.
"Now, yet another year,
it goes
on top of our tree."

      He reached
to the top
of the beautiful tree.
He placed
the gold ball
as high as he could.
"This,"
he said,
"is for Josef.
And for all the Americans
he left behind."

Thinking It Over

1. What important thing changed your thinking about something?

2. When did you ever "speak your piece"?

3. What have you ever done to show you believe in something?